Never Settle

Collected Works of

M.O. Beige

Scattered Green Galaxies Publishing

DEDICATION

TO THE GENERATIONS WHO SACRIFICED BEFORE ME.

All the works contained herein were inspired by history, current events, and mankind's neverending search for justice.

Table of Contents

The Other

I didn't know the things that you hate, could be your proudest responsibility.
I, with so much power over him,
Fear that I could be injuring, not helping
I regret not being there, even if it's impossible.
But at the same time, the annoyances he brings make him unbearable.
And seeing him in pain makes me feel like a dying rich man.
Full of fear, full of regret.
And it won't matter to me if I go through life
Standing an inch behind him,
I would take all his sorrows, and bear the cross myself.
No matter how old he gets he'll still be too young.
I, just want him to get a better chance than I did.
So I'm praying to God that he'll have empathy,
That he'll know what it's like for his family to go through life in pain.
Whatever you want, I'll give to you,
If it's my worst day or yours,
I will help you
I'll stay up all night talking to you about your troubles, and fixing
each and every one.
I want you to grow up, before you learn, not the other way around.

Chill: An Ode to Treyvon Martin

It was a dark and stormy night
Chilling at home. He left to satisfy a sweet tooth.
And when he didn't come back
A family grieves, a neighborhood mourns, a nation is baffled.
Judgment came for him packing a gun
Maybe if Judgment was colorblind
He would be home safe.
Was it because Judgment was attacked?
Did He act in self-defense?
Maybe it was because he was chilly.
And Judgment calculates his targets swiftly.
Judgment first saw, then followed, even when he was ordered to stand down.
He didn't have a chance, He was facing
on armed Judge who was profiling his face.
He ran, Judge chased after.
Thanks to his chill, Judge's stereotypes have been confirmed.
Was Judge followed?
No.
Was he in danger in any way?
Judge claimed that, "these punks always get away."
Maybe punks also get chills.
Maybe they eat skittles and tea.
And sometimes wear a hoodie.
When Judge caught Him, there was no escape.

He had a chill, walking home late,
the light rain made him pull on his hoodie
and his skin wasn't suitable
to Judge's frayed image of society,
And now, a family grieves, a neighborhood mourns,
and a nation is baffled.
And Judge walks free.
And the chill will never leave me.

Think Different

Hello? Hello?
Is anyone out there?
It's been 8 years since the monstrosities came.
And shrouded us in silence.
On June 29, 2007,
A monopolistic corporation created-
The Machines.
They sleek and cool in design.
But once you hold one, it bombards the minds
With strange and interesting images.
Swipe across, tap, tap, tap.
Siri, a snake in the grass,
bids you take a bite.
Believe everything in tweet
Believe that life is always sweet.
Makes us shy, we never have to meet
It's enslaved most of the free world.
I can't believe no one saw it coming.
An apple-bitten
C'mon, it's the forbidden
fruit.
The object which helped mankind
Fall
From being something greater.
The sign of corruption
Of too much information
Interruption.
I can feel it taking me.
The urge is too much.

Curiosity barges into my nervous system.
Taking hold of my hand.
I can't escape it!
What was Kate Upton's brother's daughter's dorm
friend's name?
I HAVE TO FIND OUT! KILL ME!
Too bad that fruit's not forbidden.
Nothing is forbidden-we all get caught in the net
We didn't need Big Brother-We got Jobs.
He just had to stick his turtleneck out for us
Body snatcher pods
They put buds in our ears, so we couldn't hear each
other screaming.
It prevents us from feeling, wondering, dreaming.
GPS of soul of the soul guides us astray
Green pigs to the slaughter, we've lost our way
We've opened Pandora's box
And got a playlist full of pestilence.
Four horsemen bring us smartphones
But make us dumb masses
With a plague of angry birds tweeting
A pestilence of pinterest
A famine of free thought
And a death of dreams.
Cause if you look it up in Soundhound
You'll get an error, sanity not found.
SO, what do we do?
Unplug, drain the batteries
Wanna-bes
Go from abuser of time to user of time
Recharge with the real
Heal-so we can feel
Again.

Soul of a Gunslinger

We are, all of us, gunslingers.
People of action, thrust into conflict without volition.
People who must learn to draw before their enemies,
or lose.
We all walk a barren desert, praying
for a cloud burst to nourish us.
Day to day, we work, to earn a living, not death.
So we don't become heat exhausted by the depression
of routine,
We dream.
Our dreams become a source of motivation
our spirits harden and become obsidian.
They form a tower.
A beacon.
A dark tower, amongst a field of roses.
So we tread this biblical desert,
to reach our tower, to be satisfied eternally, by
climbing its opal steps.
And, if seems far-fetched,
That's the point.
If dreams weren't towers,
We wouldn't even try the desert.
We choose to live, not because it is easy, but because it
is hard.
We travel with many others but still are alone.
Lone wolves, spirits, embodiments of beliefs and
experiences.
Alone, and together simultaneously,
We fight-for our Towers.

Take this L

Limerence
L-I-M-E-R-E-N-C-E
Limerence
Noun
The state of romantic attraction towards another
person
As in
I can't hide it anymore
There's something I've gotta tell you
We've been going steady for about thirty seconds
now, and I've done all the talking.
I limerence you
I know that'll become obvious, but Its gotta be clear.
I may as well be up here by myself!
I feel stronger with each phrase I spit, but weaker as
the syllables slip from my lips.
I'm too deep into this chinese finger puzzle.

Near you there's no rhyme no reason, whatever the
season, I'm feasin' to find words with meaning, don't
catch me leaning...im freezing

They say soulmates are statistically impossible
That your perfect other half would be someone who
lives near you, and not in say, Siberia.
I don't know who they is, but they need to find some
love of *they* own.

Because when you've been entrenched in this bittersweet heavenscape that the scientists call "limerence", you've already seen doubt, and jealousy, fear and loathing. And only if you literally take it to heart,
you can open Pandora's box,
and purge all the afflictions that stay locked.
Until that last emotion stays.

So yeah. I feel limerence.
You want to know how it feels?
It's looking up into the cosmos seeing the infinite everything sewn into reality,
suns that collide and form singularities,
Comets with luminescent contrails, gliding by Unknown trajectories,
shining light on shadow planets for the briefest of moments, before passing. Then you adjust your view.
Before you know it, you're not gazing up at anything, you're pinpointing the black ponds, shallow pools to the lagoon of the soul. Pupils. You're looking her in the eyes. Say something!
Uh, weather's great today, how about you?
It's saying speeches in your head but being speechless.

So when "they" use numbers and correlations to fill your Pandoras Box, give them hope. Hope that there are things we can never analyze or solve.

There are still question marks within us, unheard of
Face them before the infinite, and shove
So don't call it limerence, call it true love.

Keep it Up

We are at the crossroads, people
Don't worry, I'm not going to use my time to drop
verbal bombs against the Electors
or riddle commentary on Yeezy's state of mind.
I won't rail against the President or his hair trigger
temperament
Yeah, we need to hear these things to sow that sweet
crop of understanding.
But all too often we get fat off of scorn, off of
criticism, off prejudice.
I come with my pickaxe, to forge a stone of hope, from
our mountain of despair.
Yeah I know that was MLK, don't worry teachers I used
MLA i'd hate to plagiarize a king but, we need it.
How are you today?
Life treating you good?
You should feel good, because you got up today.
Y'all woke up,
fought the elements,
defeated your demons, and neglected fear, to be
where you are right now.
That's a miracle.
Then you take into account President Creamsicle,
the Alt- White group,
the stress of driving up here on a Saturday, and Prince
is still DEAD!
But you still woke up, and found your way here.

And you can laugh about it. Because sometimes there ain't no mountain high, ain't no adrenaline flow enough, ain't no acid ride better, than a good laugh. And, I know I'm plagiarizing again, but let me finish. You had the resilience, to live in this bipolar world, where sometimes the world seems all bleak and grey, then sometimes,

you look through it and see something that makes you laugh. Like can't breathe anymore laugh. Like fear for your life laugh.

I'm not gonna say get high on life, just take a quick hit of Serotonin.

So when you leave here, and inevitably wallow in the pit of despair (MLK), try to find somebody, a friend, mother, daughter, brother, you name it! You look them in the optic nerves, think about all that pain, about President Cheeto, about fake news, about hate, and you laugh. As hard as you can.

Abide, like the Dude.

Turn the other cheek, like Jesus.

Laugh, because it's soul food.

Let us all sit down together at the table of brotherhood, on the red hills of Georgia

Ok, too much.

Just remember, the biggest threat to your *state* of mind, is the governor.

Stay strong

Tell the dogs I'm not rolling over
and win.

Tell the courts I'm puttin you on trial
and win.

Always get through with a smile
And win

Roll past the pile of media bile
with a grin
Face the fake, don't discriminate
Cuz hate makes haste and breaks emotional weights
trapping us in crates.
I'm still standing.
We've got signs and half the world behind us.
We're still here.

Astronaut Poem

"Goodbye Houston, thanks for trying."
The static fizzles in my ear like little reapers cackling at my doom.
This, sensation of acceleration, I guess it'll be the last thing I feel.
The shuttle's white body precariously glides onto its back, and I see nothing of it but blackness.
I look above to the infinite expanse, how many have died traversing between these stars?
Brave sailors of the suns, valiant spacefaring pathfinders.
Now I join them.

8 hours until the suit is out of oxygen.
I dozed off in the suit.
Maybe I should just sleep, make it painless.
For in this sleep of death, what dreams may come?

7 hours until the suit runs out of oxygen.
The blue marble is the size of a dime.
I do wish it would just explode.
So I'd be the last one.
It's a little less depressing than having my family take the pain of knowing that I'm adrift.
I'm far enough to be off the radar,
Heh, what if some aliens were just driving along, and they just found me here and picked me up.
Buck Rogers in the 21st century.

Six hours until the suit runs out of oxygen.
The stars are more vivid now, more than I could ever
see in low orbit.
They're not just stars anymore.
They're tiny air holes that gaze into heaven.
If you go far enough, you might just break through.

Five hours until the suit runs out of oxygen.
So far, it's just like that book 2001: A I Space Odyssey.
The glory of the universe turns on every possible angle.
What was it they said in that book? About the
astronaut who drifted away and died?
"Frank Poole became the first person to reach
Jupiter."
That line always gave me chills.
I ditched the external radio.
Watched it float away.
I shouted "WILSON!" as we parted ways.
Hmm. That was a good movie.
Four hours until the suit runs out of oxygen
I can't see Earth anymore.
Fear seeds itself in my heart, and with every beat, it
roots out to the rest of my body.
I'm not afraid of death, I'm afraid of the infinite.
I, have gone further than any other living human.
I can join Tupac, Elvis, Jimmy Hoffa.

Heh, I dropped off the face of the Earth.
Three hours until the suit runs out of oxygen.
There is a god.
It's been debated on forever! But I've come to the
clear conclusion. No natural bang of atoms could
create the beauty of the infinite worlds within infinite

galaxies. Spherical islands to the unending, singularity of space.

If I don't suffocate, God will kill me, because I'm the modern Tower of Babel, heh, the engineer of NASA.

Two hours until the suit runs out of oxygen.

I've got that feeling marathon swimmers get when they lose their fear of open water.

When they're not afraid of drowning, not afraid of the sharks or piranha.

I can't tell if the moon approaching is Earth's, or Mars'.

The decompression sickness sends cramps throughout my body.

The only relaxing position feels like a crucifix.

Every time I close my eyes I can feel my mind slipping further from that titanic of sanity.

One hour until suit leaves the, what's it called? H-H2O Christ, I get it now!

I'm not dying.

I'm free!

Free to roam my melanoid utopia like a born again Adam!

Drifting not through space, but the ocean, God's ocean, and eventually I will wade through His waters searching for my own purpose! And then, I shall face the reality that lies beyond the divine diamond beach.

Is this a dream!? Because I never hope it ends!

I see! I'm going faster!

Everything's rushing past me!

Oh God! I see the planets! I made it! They line up on either side! I'm the first-

The stars are coalescing, into a mass, a ball of light at the center of my vision.

What is it? The truth?

Some alien car's headlights, coming to find me?
God's own lighthouse, run by Saint Peter, guiding me
to the beach?
My asphyxiating hallucinations?
Or is it just my desk light that I left on in the shuttle,
that my dreaming mind integrates into its story.
I zoom forward like Superman, and dive headlong into
the light...

An Ode to Ajax

Ah, who would have supposed it possible
The name I bear should ever be attuned
To these misfortunes! Doubly, trebly now
May I lament; so sore bested am I;
Whose father in Ida bore the palm once
From the whole host, and went, all-honoured, home;
BEAT While I, his son, who with no meaner power
Invaded this same tract of Troy, nor less
Myself exhibited of prowess, thus,
Being dishonoured by the Argives, perish!
And yet this much, truly, I think I know;
That if Achilles were alive, to choose
For his own arms, to whom the prize was due,
No other would have snatched it, over me.
But now the Atridae have by practice wrought
For an unscrupled villain, and passed over
The might of this right hand. Had but mine eyesight--
Had but my counsels swerved not from their aim,
Never another cause were theirs to judge
As they judged mine! 'Twas the unmastered Power,
Jove's grim-eyed daughter, that eluded me,
There as I stood, raising my hand to smite them,
Casting upon me a sick frenzy-fit,
So that my hands were reddened with the blood
Of these poor cattle! And they laugh at me!

Never settle-
To settle is to shoot down your imagination.

Father was killed in gang initiation, mother was a prostitute. Son is taken through group homes but is really raised by sports. Story follows his life from his first game to his legacy.

We see a day in his life at a foster home, and how he was raised by coaches and trainers at community center. He has odd blend of speed and strength, and is able to hold his own (but not win) against experienced wrestlers in his age group. He plays as many sports as possible to avoid being with his foster parents, who don't care about him and are willing to drop him off at his events. He plays football, does wrestling, track, but can't do fighting sports because of his age.
In middle school he does a weightlifting course with the gym teachers.
In high school, he competes at the same sports, gaining gold and glory, but finds no true friends, just faces to nod to in the hallways.
College, he is accepted on a football scholarship, he balances it with wrestling, he takes cross country and track at the college, and in his off season spars at a boxing studio.
He is infatuated with the Rocky movies.
He is a stud in college, and takes many one night stands, despite his anti-social demeanor.

Senior year he is drafted into the NFL, he signs a contract for five years.

He becomes a starting fullback when the first one becomes injured. But he also makes plays as a pass rushing linebacker. In his third and fourth year, he makes it to the pro bowl, and his fifth, he makes it to the playoffs, but not the super bowl.

The NFL begs him to stay and offers to double his pay, but he refuses, stating "It's getting old for me."

Instead of retiring, he trains at a boxing gym for a year, and signs up for the WBC. His record is 12-0, but his skill in the ring brings the world heavyweight champ call him out as a contender. He defeats him, and becomes the new champion of the world, and becomes a media sensation. He is begged to fight at least two more contenders before stepping down, to solidify his reign as champion. A gang member approaches him before the first fight and threatens to torture him if he doesn't take a dive in the fourth round. He knocks out the thug, takes his gun, and shoots at the car he came from. They drive off. He calls the police and tells them what happened. They indirectly accuse him of being affiliated with a gang, which he is disgusted by. He beats both contenders, and ends his career 15-0. His bodyguard is killed after a drive by from the same car. He leaves boxing luckily devoid of head trauma.

He moves to the east coast, and goes into Olympic Wrestling, winning gold on the global stage. An injury during a lifting session causes a doctor to tell him that all the exertion is making his body older than he is. He slips into a depression, wondering what to do with the fire that still lives inside him. So he joins the Marines, no reason other than because he needed something to do.

He serves two tours of duty. In the second, his legs are blown off from an IED. He is 35.

He gets replacements, and decides to work on his speed rather than his strength. He begins running. As his wrestling muscles begin to recede, his heart and lungs get stronger, and he realizes he has the ability to be one of the fastest people of all time. Just to be certain, he trains for three years, and makes the U.S. Olympic 100 m track team.

His score the day before he is on the world stage rivals Usain Bolt's. Feeling a sense of hubris for the first time, he chooses to walk home, claiming "I'll be home by the time you start your car." He is shot on the way home by gangbangers, but he doesn't notice until he gets home. He is able to dislodge both bullets and stop the bleeding, but he cries to himself that if he continues, he might die.

The next day, he runs nonetheless, blood slowly drips onto the track and he ignores it. He runs at top speeds, but only ties Usain Bolt. He is rushed to the hospital, where he fights off an infection for several weeks.

He retires to his mansion, and from sports altogether. He is hounded by people after his money, gangs still trying to kill him and gold diggers who don't care about him.

He is 45.

His legacy is a trail of statues, plaques, and trophies dusting on shelves.

He suffers from depression, loss of meaning.

People on interviews ask him if he was superhuman, and he doesn't respond.

The NFL calls him the 21st century Mike Singetary.
WBC calls him Clubber's strength, Drago's demeanor, and Rocky's stamina.
Wrestling says he was Milo of Croton.
The Marines say he was more marine than R. Lee Ermey.
Nonetheless, he tries to kill himself.
He is sent to the hospital, and he recovers with a psychologist, who tells him that his family troubles are over, and that the hundreds of friends he must have gained from all his sports would be glad to help him out. He goes outside to call them, but senses something bad happening. He runs into an alleyway, and sees a prostitute about to be killed as sacrifice for a gang initiation.
He crunches his knuckles and fights off the entire gang, using a mix of his lifelong skills. The prostitute escapes to call the police, but he gets stabbed, and his old wounds begin to open in front of him. One of his metal legs is broken off, and he swings it to club the gangsters. The police arrive, seeing a heap of mortally wounded gangsters, and he limps forward, towards the cop car's lights. He dreams that his legs are back, and he's running as a champion, towards a trophy marked "LIFE"
A massive crowd "it sounds like everybody in the world all together" chant his name as he runs to the trophy. And in reality he is slumped over on the police car hood.
In the end, it is ambiguous whether his wounds were quickly sealed in the hospital or whether he died where he was. But he would not be forgotten.

Hope

I drive past the neon light arch, the sign is unlit, after the EMP blast. Even though the lights are dead, I feel an illumination coming from reading the words.
I smile, my heart bangs in its chest. All my life has been leading here.
I look to Ellie, she is still sleeping in the back seat.
It's about 11:00 at night.
We're in the parking lot.
Three cars are parked.
One is a Prius, another is a Camry, and the last is a motorcycle.
I can tell that no one beat us here.
Screw the parking lot.
I drive through, following the trail of old golf carts, to the ticket stand.
I roll through the barricades, crunching metal under the wheels.
Driving past an alley of stores and shops, I know we have food for months.
In the distance looms the castle, only about three hundred yards up.
A tear rolls down my cheek.
I keep driving, the moon at our backs.
The castle is now only feet away.
I giggle under my breath.
Ah, here we go.
Only feet away from it.

I get out of the truck, it's freezing, but, luckily this area hasn't been congregated, at least, not to an overwhelming degree.

I lock the doors on the truck.

I walk in, toting the M4 Carbine I got off the dead Atlanta National Guardsman.

His final position suggested it was a faithful gun.

I first check the gift shop, looking away from the charred stuffed animals and plaster dust in the air.

No one.

A noise goes off behind me.

I swing around, leaning the rifle back, in preparation to stab someone with the Ka-Bar Knife on the front.

A music box opened, and was spitting out moldy notes, where it used to be a lovely symphony.

It sounded like "Someday my Princess will Come for You", or whatever the hell they called it, it was in a Disney movie, Sleeping Beauty I think.

Ellie would know what it was.

All clear.

I take the head flashlight, turn it on, and walk slowly up the drafty staircase.

Second floor, we could sleep here tonight, but no no no,

I care for my princess too much.

Nothing but chateaus and a dining hall, full of rusted silverware and fine china shattered to dust.

Old paintings where the oil has run out.

All clear.

I continue up the stairs,

this is the good part.

Third floor.

Members only. I joke.

The room, is beautiful.
Staggeringly, even by the dim light sourced by a couple
of D batteries,
it is heartwarming.
Climactic,
Poetically justified.
Perfect.
I guessed there was a visitor a couple of days before
the first bomb.
And the staff cleaned the place up.
I check the room, making sure not to hide my
thoroughness in the face of eagerness.
All
clear!
I race down the stairs.
Half-crying from relief as I do.
I check the truck,
no more monsters.
I pick up Ellie, cradling her in my arms.
She stirs, but stays asleep.
She was pretty burnt out the other day.
I carry her up the damp steps, which now feel
glistening with renewal.
Second floor,
third floor.
We're here.
I lay her down in her king-size bed.
She shakes a little from the cold.
I lay a blanket over her.
Job's not done yet.
I brought the water jugs from the truck up.
And a couple lanterns.
And the guns.

If any Blood Boys get the truck, they're only getting the half tank of gas to go with it.

I clean the guns by her side, the sun beginning to poke out of the ground, shedding light on my old troubles, and bringing forth new hopes.

"Joseph?" She grumbles.

She gasps, slowly waking up and noticing her surroundings.

"Joseph. Where. The Hell. Are. We?"

"Where dreams come true, baby."

A tear rolls out of her eye.

"I know you wanted to take the vacation here, and with, you know, society in the way, we couldn't pay the bills."

She jumps up and hugs me, crying into my shoulder.

I hug her back, I feel like crying too.

"I love you Joseph."

"I love you too Eliza."

If all this nuclear crap blows over, and they make a movie about our story, the ending should be of us, hugging right where we are, and the camera pans out of the window, out into the distance, so the audience can see the twist,

We're in Disney World.

Cinderella Castle to be precise.

And they all lived happily ever after.

New Clear Mission

"MUSH!" Lars bellows, his Santa Claus belly jiggling in the icy air.

The snow treads by as the ten dogs work their best to get us away from the blizzard.

The valley expands as we move further down. The blinding snow emphasizes the empty flat grounds we ride over.

Lars gives out a hearty laugh as the dogs speed up.

It's hard to be comfortable where I am. Not just in the sleigh, but with the world. San Francisco being nuked? I'm surprised we're still alive.

"Leonard! You take the reins, give it a try."

Lars hands the leather belts to me.

"No, no, no... I said I wanted the backseat tour!"

"Nonsense! Give yer wife something to talk about when we get back!"

His mittened hands shove the reins into mine.

My hands are literally frost bitten, I fumble with the ropes and eventually get a good grip.

Numbness is still there, which means I haven't had nerve damage (I think).

"If you want them to move, you have to really pull it back, so they'll feel it and get the idea." His Ahab-esque voice sends tremors through my skull.

I say something like "Got it." But muffled.

I shift back hard, sending the dogs into a slanted left turn.

Careful Leonard, don't over correct. I think to myself.

"Ye've got it!" He slaps me hard on the back, which sends a flat sheet of stinging pain north of my spine. The dogs begin to slow down, and after twenty feet, they've completely halted.

Crap, what did I do?

The dogs huddle together and whimper.

"I... I'm sorry, what did I do?" I stammer.

Lars is already off the sleigh, he doesn't turn to me as he speaks. "Nothing wrong at all, they've been spooked, must be that sixth sense animals got."

I gulp and look around my shoulder. "Wolves?"

"No, we'd have seen them coming in an empty valley like this." Lars gets down on one knee and pets the dogs, his full beard nuzzling a malamute's ear.

I look to the sky, something is falling, little yellow flashes of light are falling out of the sky, with Aurora Borealis being the backdrop.

"L-Lars?"

He turns, wordless, and sees.

"Mayhap a meteor shower?"

"Nukes." I choke out.

"Nay, there's too many, and, they all can't be headed this direction."

The dogs howl, in fear? Mourning? What?

The yellow lights do look like meteors, but they're moving too slow. I can't explain it, they're breaking up, splitting apart like cells.

Burning up in the atmosphere.

They soar across the air for a good ten minutes before they disappear.

"Let's go, we'll figure it out at the home."

With that, Lars returned to the helm, and mushed us home.

Maria kissed me on the cheek when we returned, and we all got some hazelnut coffee.

On CNN, they reported a government whistleblower who had stated that we had lost contact with the International Space Station. And that Russia was building up a massive coalition to absorb Ukraine, Kazakhstan, and Uzbekistan.

"War's coming folks." Lars says solemnly. "I think it'd be safe to miss yer flight tomorrow and stay here, for awhile."

"Lars, the shooting stars we saw, could it have been-"

"No. I doubt it." Lars says, trying to end the conversation.

The International Space Station probably, crashed a few miles short of Nome. Jesus, how many people are on board that thing?

If war is coming, Alaska will be Omaha Beach for the Russians. Oh God. Where do we go?

Maria sees the fear in my eyes and eases her hand into mine. She always calms me down, puts me at ease. I sigh deeply. We'll make it.

Somehow.

The sub commander's brisk "Fire." ended all hope for Oleg. He pressed the button, and the president had unlocked the missiles.

The men on the Oscar II submarine began singing. It was an orthodox hymn. There was a rumble, and a shake, and it was over. Sineva swam to the surface and breached the water, travelling through the sky at an angle only a computer could produce.

Sineva had eventually gone suborbital. She flew through the airless space, coldly and without word. A series of calculating clicks set off inside her metal skin, changing her course, gravity supporting her descent. She screamed like a teapot.

Some of the Russian inscriptions on her body were peeling off from the sheer acceleration.

She had reached her destination. Thousands of people exited their cars, hearing the sirens and warnings, but stood catatonic, for their impending doom.

Sineva kissed the black asphalt. Her engine collided with the ground before the real damage was done. A ball of fire rose from Sineva's corpse in less than a second. It expanded to feet in diameter, then meters. Then it rose to the sky, releasing heat to all miles around. 30 miles away people received full body sunburns in a second. People at ground zero were dust.

The shockwave hit then. Cars flew into buildings like hail, and anything not based with concrete blew away like a card castle against a fan. The White House was a pile of toothpicks in the wind, the Capitol set fire, and vaporized. The Washington Monument's base stood against the force, but the top half flew away. Not a scream to be heard, except for Sineva's destructive death rattle.

When the waves of fire and shock had ceased, there was silence. The city was, in ancient terms, salted, nothing else would grow there, ever again.

Smaller cities in all directions were burned, all glass had shattered, but some still survived. Soon Sineva's lifeblood would be sent up with the wind, and into the clouds, and would begin to poison everything on Earth.

The President watched the everything in soul-crushing guilt, from his bunker in Cheyenne Mountain.

North Korea finally does it. They drop an ICBM on San Francisco, expecting surrender.

The U.S. president is a careful one, there's no Mutually Assured Destruction, North Korea is assaulted by U.S. and South Korean forces along the DMZ, but there's no invasion.

Three days pass between the San Fran bombing and the retaliation.

Day 1. The U.S. military is completely mobilized for war, no reserve forces are called upon yet. North Korea celebrates the attack, and Russia's leaders, seeing a plan to bring back the old regime, plan to make an alliance with North Korea, China, and several other countries.

Day 2. The initial reaction in the U.S., citizens mourn and prepare for global war, many gun stores throughout the nation are ransacked, and many, dig, to make nuclear shelters. San Francisco is still intact, and emergency services such as NEST arrive for aid. America's allies fear the oncoming attack and cut all ties, countries such as Great Britain, Germany, and France drop away. Japan stays loyal and prepares citizens and military for nuclear strike.

Day 3. Russia, China, and North Korea make up a new defense coalition, nuclear weapons are armed and ready all over the world. The coalition instantly begins invading neighboring countries like Kazakhstan, Mongolia, Kyrgyzstan, Tajikistan, Uzbekistan, Ukraine, Georgia, and Turkey. The assault is so massive in size that many nations instantly submit. Resistance forces are only opposition. Russia is so focused on the coalition that they put nukes off the table, but North Korea launches another missile for Seattle, and the U.S. attacks.

After the 3rd day, the U.S. launches all nukes, landing and obliterating:

Moscow (airburst)

Beijing (airburst)

Kiev (ground burst for fallout effect)

Pyongyang (ground burst for fallout effect)

many other cities.

America's allies fire as well, hoping to destroy the coalition before it can fire. Nukes turn the China-North Korean border into a no man's land. The DMZ is fought for with tooth and nail by a united force of Japanese, South Korean, and U.S. soldiers. On the fifth day, a Russian flotilla enters New York Harbor, but the invasion force is quickly subdued by an already paranoid and vigilant New York Police, National Guard, and even citizens. The Russians drop a hitherto top secret modern variant of the Tsar Bomba on Washington D.C,., turning the city, and all of Northern Virginia to dust, and the fallout kills millions southbound on the eastern seaboard. The U.S. president is safely hidden underground, somewhere in the Midwest. On the sixth day, U.S. submarines launch their ICBMs, and turn the remainder of the North Korean forces into ash, Surviving U.S., Japanese, and South Koreans begin entering the country to liberate people in the concentration camps, no one is left. India and Pakistan both go off the map, and no communications can be established with either. Russians send out their nuclear arsenal against the U.S., Western Europe, and Japan.

The U.S., Japanese, and South Koreans meet up with soldiers from Australia, and all forces in the Pacific unite against any opposition, planning to destroy Russia and any remains of the wrecked Chinese government, calling themselves the United Pacific Offensive, they are now the only functioning government in Asia. The Offensive marches through Siberia, planning to hit Moscow soon.

The U.S. is somewhat intact, with the Blood Boys cult rapidly growing in popularity in the martial state of NEw York City. The Blood Boys soon gain enough influence to overpower the military, and eventually travels the world, preaching their sadistic message of control to Africa, the Mediterranean nations, and the Middle East. They meet up with the weary Offensive in Moscow, and their forces quickly take them down. The Skirmish in Moscow, would become the point where the Blood Boys rule the world, politically and militarily. It has been two months since San Francisco has been nuked.

Any people left either fend for themselves or submit to the now industrial Blood State.

There is no hope.

E Pluribus Me

Character who has never been president. Believes politics aren't about opinions. Hardass who manipulates.

Self proclaimed narcissist. Played by silver haired 50ish thin caucasian, sporting Henry Kissinger glasses, should be somewhat attractive. (Jon Stewart could do, if he aged a bit),

"I don't call it bossiness, I prefer "enhanced leadership towards the weak.""

Goes to gun shop and buys whole stock of weapons. Clerk asks why he needs them.

"I don't know, the same bull*&%^ excuse we've used since the 1790s, um, it's my right?"

"O.J. Simpson's lawyer is proof that Heaven exists and uses Guardian Angels."

"My father was a conservative man. He said f*%# society, f@#% morality, do what your heart says. I loved my father, he was a rare alcoholic, you know, those ones that don't abuse you."

Proposed eight times, rejected seven times. The eighth wanted the marriage as a green card so she could enter the country, and later gun down House Reps. If it weren't for the Texan Senator and his concealed RPG-7, many more would be dead.

Takes journalist student under his wing, becomes his campaign manager.

Has fetish for secretaries.

In attempt to seem more powerful, he hired a mercenary to shoot him at the beginning of a speech, just so he could finish the speech before going to hospital, but passes out after two minutes.

Born on a casino table in Vegas, a $100 chip plopped on his head, since then, he had been graced with the miracle of greed.

Father was Attorney General, which is why his son was graced with ultra-debate.

"We are here live at the Virginia Primary, about to listen to Marlon Atticus, Senator of the state, and

considered by many to be the Kanye West of American politics. Let's see what he has to offer us today."
Marlon stepped on stage.
"Hello, my fellow Americans (and Agnostics). My father, was a dri... My father was a connosieur of whiskey. He was one of those people who would be intoxicated, but never lay a hand on their children. He once told me
"Son, fuck society, fuck morality, do what your heart says."
I loved my father. He, as you all might know, was Attorney General for several years. He was my inspiration, and he will be missed, by me, a few free con men, and four D.C prostitutes."
The moderator spoke, "Senator, what do you plan to do if you become president?"
"I shall adopt new gun control legislation, the only one legally allowed to own a firearm in the country is me. I am also willing to turn away my old promise of installing martial law in cities such as LA, Detroit, and New York City. I will now only do this in places I visit, to give myself a more Big Brother appeal."
"Are there any questions for Mr. Atticus?"
A news woman in a red suit jumped up.
"Yes, Clara Dalton, ABC News illegal copyright website, there have been rumors lurking around that you have an irrational fear of Furbies, is this true?"
"Excellent question, where did you hear these rumors?"
"Well, if you'll remember two years ago, a video was leaked showing a whistleblower holding a Furby near you, and the camera panned to your terrified face."

Marlon couldn't move. He had talked himself out of abduction and into murder, but he felt that he couldn't walk away from this.

"The allegations...are...mis..."

Misguided?

Misjudged?

Miscarriaged?

"Misunderstood! I was terrified in the video because I couldn't believe that the Furby was running on Lithium-Ion batteries, instead of a clean electric charge, because, and to brag, I am an environmentalist, again to the extent that the planet can be helped, but also still screwed."

Everyone applauded, he felt like he had hit a home run, without steroids!

"But Senator, you say in the video and I quote, "No please get that demented monster away from me I beg of you, take my children instead, oh Jesus that demented thing.""

Marlon perspirated, good thing he was wearing armpit sponges.

"I was referring to the whistleblower madam, the whistleblower who had given away government secrets and made America susceptible to attack, and I just couldn't stand him."

More applause, one man did a tearful salute.

America in Three Parts

Part I
I am from history.
I am from leadership and warfare and dispute.
I am from outdoors and wind and crumpled leaves.
I am from the sweet smell of pollen, and the
remembrance of conflict.
I am from long hours of study, and its reward.
I am from Elizabeth and Emmanuel.
I am from Africa and Italy and much more, and I wear
pride like a medal.
I am from silence.
I am from cooperation and "get back on the horse"
and commitment.
I am from rebellion.
I am from patriotism and deep passion for culture.
I am from transforming dreams into the truth.
I am from "what doesn't kill you makes you stronger"
I... Am... America.

Shangri-La Part II
The bullets fly over my head like hummingbirds fly
around a flower.
Machine gun nests cloak the streets, there must be
thousands of enemy soldiers.
My squad is cowering in a derelict shop at the other
side of the street.
But I must focus, or I'll die.

Leaning out of my cover, I flick the pin off a grenade and toss it like an excited boy tossing his first baseball. Then I go into the fetal position, covering my ears and shutting my eyes.

Then, the ground seems to be trying to lift me off of it as the loudest bang I've ever heard in this war rings out throughout the block.

It was so loud I swear people from Iowa would hear it as well.

After the enemy fumbles out of their holes, they feed more ammunition into their guns and fire again

I am frustrated.

I jump up and begin shooting my Thompson towards them.

I scream and slam my eyes shut.

Then suddenly, silence.

I open my eyes and see not the hellish catacomb I was at before,

but a valhalla.

I walk on clouds and see a long glorious waterfall frothing out of a cloud bank.

It was so beautiful it would make any cold hearted man fall on his knees and cry, renouncing all his sins.

I look down and see a battlefield,with people shooting one another.

One person is shot and a transparent silhouette of his corpse rises into the sky, up to where I am

A golden gate opens and just now I ask myself "Am I dead?"

Part III

America, seven letters and four syllables of beauty,
born from a 1,137 word document that "declared" her
birth;
She's a lighthouse in the stormy ocean of the world;
We settled the west like a nail settles into a board;
We fought for her with booming cannon and white
knuckles;
We changed the way we see her, not by whips and
labor, by equality;
We are like David, battling Goliath, we are strong when
we believe in ourselves;
Imagine being a vagrant in a rotten alleyway in Europe,
and turning to the hustle and bustle of New York City;
We struggle for peace, as we are an argumentative
people;
But we change the lava of conflict into a "stone of
hope";
Gorgeous, galvanizing, guile, and gallant.
She is so powerful, so inspirational, she is treated as a
person;
She's helped us get to the Moon, get to equality, and
get to speak out;
Natural Americans are brave when someone insults
her;
We have developed a leadership mindset from her
affection, her ability to do the impossible, her place in
the world.

Inside Outer Reach

My creativity reaches no bounds,
like a factory, turning metal to masterpiece.
I am a leader, a fighter, a lover,
Persevering to projects beyond my level,
like a curious little child, seeing the stars for the first
time.

Writing to me,
is like a funnel,
it takes the art and grand beliefs and insights of my
mind,
and shrinks it down to fit on a piece of paper.

I the patriot.
yearning to be a leader
defend my country,
A cat, only deadly when provoked.

My absolute greatest compliment would be "hero",
I want to be the shield, blocking off attacks from those
I love.

I know peace is much better than war,
but peace is the hardest thing to achieve in this world,
no matter how pacifist we get,
there will always be someone out there ready to pull
the trigger,
to start the fight, and he will always exist,
like the toughest kid on the block,

ready to prove his strength at the slightest
encouragement.

My determination is the only form of bravery I have,
determination to win, is all I need to survive.
The only greater cause I could get behind is
exploration,
I want desperately, as a small child wants Santa to be
real, to go to space.
To be far from home, and fording Humanity's next
step.

The perfect society in my opinion,
is that of the Native Americans,
their hunter-gatherer routine guaranteed food for all,
health for all, and no scarcity,
an Eden, plucked away by the Europeans.

I am not stubborn (at least I've not heard anything to
the contrary)

To be honest, I don't see the glass as half empty or half
full,
I say "who drank from my glass!?"
"That's gross!"

Introverted near strangers
extroverted near friends, (as we all are)
okay with being alone
love being with others.

Rorschach Test

Two vast warring empires, connected under the same
roof.
They are locked in everlasting conflict, why?
Human nature, it always boils to war.
Above ground the two worlds collide,
firing their anti-gravity weapons and smashing each
other with their dotted bullets.

Beneath, a steampunk fantasy,
ages of industrial growth
the only remnants of the peoples once prominent tech
boom.
Both large empires are named, not Montague and
Capulet,
but you might find this as a nickname.

Is this world ours?

Perhaps, we may be the authors of this destruction.

Is this but a window into a grimmer future?

Definitely.

This world is dying, and not even the most intelligent
of men can end it.
With any hope, someone will reach out to the middle,
look inside, and find peace.

The Fall of the House of Rusher

Robert never believed he was a "bad" person; he understood why people could believe him to be "bad", of course, it's to-may-to to-mah-to. What some called bigotry he called the divine right to hate niggers. He couldn't stand them. Oh, he could take those Pollacks, those Orientals, hell, he even had sympathy for the Red man. But no, he despised the niggers more than George Wallace ever did. Robert's family even hosted the lynchings back until '65.

Robert stood outside of his house, sweat on his brow, on his knees, staring into the crawlspace, mystified. It was a black hole, with no indicator of depth being found. He yelled into it, and his voice had no echo, it didn't bounce around the hitherto five-foot-deep ditch like usual, He reached down with a stick, and couldn't reach anything. Hell, even the match he dropped down the was swallowed by the emptiness.

"Did you know Robert, that this house used to be a church?" The pastor asked.

"My folks said it was a one room chapel before they built it up."

"Yes, it started slightly submerged, the crawlspace was the original floor. My father went there every Sunday as a boy. He told me that that place was magical, that some sort of energy emanated about it, he even remembered hearing a faint buzzing sound, like a bee buzzing, and a sense of peace that other churches just didn't generate."

"I wouldn't know about that, we never heard buzzing, not since we added the second floor."

"Yes, I have a radical theory about this. When my father attended church, our town was out of the loop, all we knew was that the commies were going to drop nukes on us any second. And generally, I'm sure everyone and their mother believed that Heaven didn't seem that far after the nuclear war. So, people went to church, confessed their sins, got themselves "cleaned up" for the Lord. The hope to go to Heaven probably brought out people's bare, naked souls."

"So what'cher sayin' here is that my family don't have souls?!"

"Not in the slightest, but to completely renovate a house of God does raise questions…"

"Get da fuck out of my house! Don't be raising questions about my pure family! My parents were married!" Kaji barked violently at his master's exclamation.

With that, the priest was shoved from the house, and the door slammed in his face. The bang of the door closing sounded more like a beast closing its jaws on prey more than anything else. Rob went to bed soon after.

Robert opened his eyes unto a plantation. Surrounded by a jungle of prickly cotton plant, each stalk about six feet tall. His tan yet still pale skin became one of darkest brown. The Georgia sun beat down upon his neck, feeling like acid, cooking his entire strange body to a sweaty exterior.

"SAM! WHERE THE HELL ARE YA!?" The unmistakable accent, deep booming voice, drunken slur, it sounded like his grandpappy.

He took notice of his skin's pigment, and was shocked nearly to tears. This had to be a dream.

"SAM! GODAMMIT! SHOW YOURSELF YOU BASTARD! MAKING ME WALK HERE IN THE HEAT WITH NOTHING BY MY OVERALLS!

Rob was frozen in fear. His grandpappy would execute swift and merciless injustice upon him, nigger or not. The rumpling leaves grew closer.

Rob backed into the thicket.

"I HEAR YOU BOY!"

Rob began to sprint, the cotton pricks slicing at his shirtless skin. He let out a scream of agony, in the nigger's voice of course.

Grandpappy grabbed him by the shoulders, threw him to the ground, and began kicking his body with his weathered, firm boot, like a woodsman chopping a tree. The pain ripped away at him, he could take no more.

"Grandpappy! Stop! I'll do anything!"

The strong fifty-year-old man pulled him to his feet with one hand.

"You want help?! THEN CONFESS!"

The hand squeezed tighter around Rob's neck.

"CONFESS OR BE DAMNED!"

Rob screamed himself out of his dream. He had sweat through all his clothes. It was around eleven in the morning. Kaji was pawing at him, surprised. Rob got out of bed, drew himself a hot bath, and ate breakfast. Kaji gobbled up his food as if it was his last meal. Little did Rob know that he had been asleep for two days under the nightmare.

Hello operator? Get the police. You see, I can't get out of my house, and my dog has gone wild. Rob continued wrapping his arm with the white surgical cloth, blood stained it immediately. It sounded like wind blew over the phone. The kind you hear in those movies where there's a tornado, or a sandstorm. The sound reminded him of a childhood dream of hell, a dry, desolate blood swamp, and the wind howled so emptily

It sounded like falling.
It sounded like a something charging, screaming.

Kaji barked and banged at the door downstairs. Rob hoped he locked strong enough. Was it rabies that made the retarded mutt bite him? No, he'd know if it was. Kaji just jumped out and bit him, if he hadn't thrusted his hand out to cover the dog's face, he'd have his throat ripped open.

Confess or die?

Confess to what?

Rob's memory flushed back to when James got locked up for "hate" crimes, when he came out he was trying to talk about all the races being together.

"I'm not confessin' to shit!" He yelled to no one.

Was it night? It looked like night, the sky was black, but he had woken up but two hours ago- it was summer, it should be bright as blazes.

Oh damn! The window! He thought. He unlatched the window. The drop was quite a bit far, but he decided he would make it. He got the emergency chain ladder from under his bed. He latched it on and began climbing down. He weighed about 200 pounds, good for his size. He dropped down two rungs from the bottom, and turned his head to the crawlspace, still black, still mesmerizing. Rob heard a buzz, but not anything soothing. It sounded like a bee buzzing, circling a little boy's frightened head. It sounded nothing like the pastor's description, a buzz of happiness, a buzz of God's will. No, it sounded like some

new

thing.

Rob saw a flash across his vision, it was so horrific his mind hadn't grappled what the hell it was. It

s

felt like heat, but

o

had a more malevolent

u

power to it, like a kid

l

holding a gun.

Rob didn't like this. It was too much.

He sprinted over to the shed, took out his father's camouflaged Olympia, and a box of ammo.

Why did he need it?

He wouldn't shoot Kaji, never. Maybe just bat him with the gun if worst came to worst.

He just felt, instinct, plucking at his brain.

Something is not right.

Bad things here.

A twig snapped, some miles away, and he heard it.

Then two twigs.

Then more.

From miles away, invisible roots were yanked and
pulled out long threads of sound.
Coming closer.
"Fuck this." Rob rushed back to the ladder.
His head moved without his orders, it snapped to the
crawlspace. The buzzing sound was louder.
"SHUT UP! YOU AND ALLOTHOSE OTHERS!"
The buzz turned into a churn.
It sounded like a waterfall frothing, louder and louder.
Rob snapped.
He fired both shots of the Olympia into the crawlspace,
screaming.
The bullets seemed to echo in the space, making the
sound stop.
Then start again, making an aggressive buzzing sound,
and
firing not the bullets,
but the bullet sound back at him.
The sound knocked him to his feet, sending a wild echo
through the woods, making the twig-snapping-
invisibleroot sound hit to a sprint. Rob jumped up to
the ladder, neglecting the shotgun on the ground.

Damn was Rob tired. Facing down nightmares, a
potential rabies infection, the supernatural, and maybe
even God beats the strength out o' ya. Kaji had gone
quiet, Rob could hear him snoring, leaned against the
door.
Rob tried the phone again.
"HELLO? Police, please for the love of God, PICK UP!"
The scary wind noise was all that replied.
Followed by a
clicking sound.

Like a cemetery gate swinging open.
And the wind
got louder.
Rob slammed the receiver shut.
The house creaked, or "settled" as his parents told him.
Rob grabbed the bible under his bed.
CONFESS
Rob could hear the air of the voice on his neck, little hairs stood up there as he flew around, sure as Mary was a virgin that someone was there.
No crickets chirped as the last photons drained from the world outside Rob's window. He looked out, the shotgun was no longer visible, the ladder was halfway there, as if it cut off into nothingness where the ground met it. The walls of the house shone extremely bright against the dark, like his house was a star and the world was space.
If there was a threshold where fear reaches a point where it can move your bowels, Rob had driven a coast to coast trip past it. Had he eaten anything today, he would need a change of clothes. But he didn't eat, so his fear was made audible with some light flatulence.
"Confess to what?!"
The darkness seemed to absorb the sound, the silence was deafening.
Downstairs, he heard skittering along the floor. Kaji heard it and awoke, not answering with barks of defense, but of eager yips of joy, like his owner came home.
Rob was hungry, fighting back wave upon wave of stomach groans. He learned to see with his ears.
Skitter

Skitter
Baby
killer.
Kaji was gone, left the stairs, and probably moved to get something to eat.
The skitter was nearby, pacing back and forth near the stairs like a sentry in the night.
Rob forgot to turn off the power, and with his weak generator, all the lights would be out within two days.
And
then
they'll
kill
me.
Stop it! There's a rat out there, that's it.
Nothing but a massive
furry
black
rat.
Kaji probably got spooked by it.
Rob set up a trap, should anyone claw the door open and run up the stairs to get him, he placed an elaborate system of wooden crates, armed with thick splinters, triggered by a tripwire in the middle of the stairs.
Rob comforted himself, saying that he would be safe, and went to sleep.
Ain't it nice that the human mind can blatantly lie to itself and believe it?
In the morning, (if it could be called that) the crow of a rooster was replaced with a banshee's screech, it sounded a mile or so out.
I need that gun. Now. Rob knew.

He carried with him, a tire iron, lodged in his back pocket. A tear rolled down his cheek as he went over the ladder, into the darkness. Each rung was a whimper from him. The world got darker and darker as he went down. The white glow of the house seemed distant and far, like a light at the end of a tunnel. And then he touched the ground.

Rob screamed in his mind at first, but it grew to a scream of joy, fear, and regret all at once. He got on his hands and knees, moving his hands all over the darkness for the dropped weapon. As one hand clutched the gun, his other hand was grabbed by

a

cold

wet

paw.

Rob never screamed so loud in his life. He scrambled up the ladder, neglecting the gun again. His scream changing to a frustrated laugh as he was halfway up. Then he heard the trap get sprung. A banshee shriek of pain resounded in the room.

Rob could only see the window's edge, nothing inside. A heavy burst of air whooshed into him.

Rob likened it to a large bird passing by.

The skitter had set off the trap.

He could hear it in his room.

It didn't take long for it to begin to jiggle the ladder.

No

Then it shook the ladder ferociously, screeching as it did.

Rob heard the pitter patter of Kaji's paws scampering up the stairs.

Rob knew it wouldn't hold, he clutched the corner of

the building, and grabbed hold of the bricks on the steeple of the house. The ladder was forcefully yanked into the window, followed by enraged screeches, ripping up the metal ladder into bits.

Rob decided to take shelter, he couldn't take this anymore. He would reside in the tiny church belfry until...

Until what?

"I don't know, until this is over."

It won't ever be...

"Stop it!"

Rob slowly climbed up to the belfry. He got several footholds on loose bricks as he reached the thick roof. As he walked around, trying to remember where he was in the pitch-dark night (if it was night). He saw a tiny glimmer of white in the water of black. As he walked towards it, he felt a monster bird wind blow past his back. He got goosebumps.

Rob saw movies, he knew not to look back when stalked.

He instead walked faster, whispering sweet hymns to himself to stay

alive.

sane.

Rob felt it, whether it's instinct or telepathy or morphic resonances, or just the circumstances, he knew it. He pictured a pterodactyl, glowing fire red, with quarter sized eyes and a man-sized beak, gunning for him. Swooping down to snatch him up like a

pelican

and a fish. Rob saw the pterodactyl diving for him in his mind's eye. So, he turned, and quickly saw it in his eye's eye. He ducked, and rolled to the side of the roof, too disconcerted to speak.

CRACK!

The pterodactyl stabbed into the roof and flew around for another pass.

Rob didn't see anything except the tiles of broken roof flying in all directions.

Next time won't be lucky.

Rob whimpered as he jumped back up, sprinted forward, and quickly clambered into the belfry tower. He closed the four glass windows and took a deep breath.

"Now what?"

We try to live. Find food, DON'T go outside, get a gun.

"The shotgun was all we had."

Bull

shit.

You have more guns, and you know it. Where are they.

The glass window opened,

a bloody hand holding it

followed by an eyeless, bug infested head poking through.

"Gon' die tonight baby!"

Rob screamed as his innards were slurped up like spaghetti by the monster.

And then he opened his eyes.

A dream? All of it?

No-

just the head and arm part.

He was still in the belfry, it had been a half hour since the pterodactyl came.

Rob looked through the window with remorse

He saw nothing, but heard

the invisbleroot snap sound, it combined with the wind and formed a sort of audible beast, a biped, whose steps were a combination of gruesome noises, bones snapping like carrots, skin ripped like a wet blanket.
As the beast took a step, there was a rumble.
The entire house shook.
Kaji howled below him.
Rob took up a cross in the belfry. He held it close to him and stopped looking out the window.
Step.
Crash.
His dishes broke from the tremor.
Rob could swear that he would see something that sounded that large. He looked out the window again.
The eyeless head peered out at him, its remainders of a face smooshed into the window.
Rob screamed.
The cross kept him safe.
"GON' DIEEE TONIGHT! GON' DIE IF YOU DON'T CONFESS!"
"Confesss?" Rob whimpered.
"niggerS ROBERT! SAVE YOURSELF! HURTING niggerS IS HURTING YOUR SOUL! GON' GO TO HELL IFFIN YOU DON'T CONFESS!"
The eyeless head scuffled off on its frail yet fast body, into the dark.
Ain't that just divine?
Divine intervention.
The army, navy and marines of Hell all here to make you love negroes.
Rob did a grumble laugh.
"When did niggers do ME any good? They just destroy 'emselves with gangs and Hennessy."

So did your dad.
Rob hadn't heard that voice before.
It was the voice of logic.
He tried to shun it out.
To no avail.
They were forced here.
Shut up.
Those niggers have more than every right to be treated fairly.
SHUT UP!
It did.
Survival instinct kicked in.
Look for weapons.
A hammer.
Rob sighed in victory cradling the rubber handle.
Something told him that he didn't have time to be afraid, he thought, no
he felt that, he was falling somewhere,
To Hell.
Quiet, not there.
You know it's true.
The skitter was in the bedroom, he just needed to bring Kaji there.
Then, he'd close the door on both of them,
Take the car
and drive off
You know, go off Pandemonium Avenue, take a left at the Damnation Turnpike, and ride Route 666 all the way home.
Do you have any better ideas?!
Silence.
Yeah bitch, I thought so.
Rob opened the belfry door in the floor.

The dark wasn't normal, it was more like tendrils of black, like a fog, drifting around him, wanting to pull him in but couldn't.

Rob set his left foot on the ladder, and started down. There were eight rungs.

1

This is bad.

2

Mommy? Where are you, I don't want to go down here.

3

He was still somewhat in the belfry, but the black was all consuming.

The only illumination was a trickle of light from the belfry windows.

4

The dark was so powerful.

So awe-inspiringly empty, and full at the same time.

Empty of hope

Full of

M

O

N

S

T

5

E

R.

Shut up!

I feel like I'm going insane.

6

Rob couldn't

see

anything.
If a nigger wore purple overalls and juggled condoms
with a lantern
and was a foot away from him
He wouldn't see it.
Rob laughed.
It was no tiny restrained chuckle.
Or normal fart reaction.
This was a belly laugh.
A deep laugh.
A no holds barred, lock me up in the nuthouse
CUCKOO CACHOO
MAD HATTER laugh.
Rob couldn't stop it.
He started crying too.
He saw an image flash in his head.
He didn't know if he made it or if it was something
else.
It was his body
Blood lapped up by Kaji
organs smashed into goo
His head, still intact, but separated from the neck.
laughing his ass off.
This image made him laugh harder.
But inside he didn't want to laugh.
Another image
His headstone.

> Here lies Robert Rusher
> One inbred country hick
> Found hairless, eyeless, dickless
> Laughing his dumb ass off.
> We miss him dearly.

Rob screamed in laughter.

Then he heard the skitter, coming down the stairs.
He pissed himself laughing.
5
He found it all so painful
4
The skitter was in the room now.
Rob didn't look down.
But he knew it was at the base of the belfry ladder,
just looking at him.
3...
Something clawed at his leg.
The claws at were cold as ice.
As they nicked his skin.
Like getting cut by an icicle.
2,
1.
The claw let go of his leg almost instantly.
It was a scare tactic.
Rob was reeling from the laughter,
tears going down his face in streams.
Reduced to slight giggles.
The skitter imitated his laugh, perfectly.
Like a microphone would.
But the laugh sounded gargled.
Like he was laughing in a sea of liquid.
Not blood,
at least not human blood.
Rob looked down the belfry chamber.
He SAW the skitter.
It had wrinkled eyeholes.
An aged face.
A paper white face.

teeth so big that the face was trapped in an eternal grin.
and a naked mole like shape.
But it spoke in a deep tenor so powerful Rob was sure it was on steroids.
"M
A
A
A
A
A
A
A
A
A
A

A
A
N
!"
Rob slammed the belfry door shut.
Then, out of the most retarded
dum
dum
curiosity.
Rob opened it again.
The skitter was right behind the door.
"I AM DEATH!"
Rob cackled furiously with laughter
and passed out.
Leaving the door wide open.
As he slept

he laughed.
And another thing laughed beside him.
and another
and another.
Till his brain was crammed with nothing but maniac
laughing of all monsters and ghouls.
And he couldn't hear his own voice, but he was sure he
was screaming now.

He awoke.
Sweat and piss stained his entire body.
Rob cried, his tears smelling odd.
He was crying black liquid.
He closed his eyes,
slammed his fists shut.
and begged the end of it.
His heart couldn't take it.
The eyeless corpse was at the window again.
"Robertttttttttttttttttttttttttttttttttttt"
Rob didn't really feel up for defending himself
anymore.
"What?"
"I'm like you. A hater of other races. I was in the same
situation as you. AND I jumped Out the window, into
the darkness. Don't do what I DID, your soul leaps out
of you, leaving you alive and begging for someone."
"Help me."
"You have to find God."
"In here?"
"God is everywhere. He's got friends in high places, or
in this case, low places. He hE ha HA!"
"Where am I?"

"You're on an elevator to hell, but you're stuck between floors. God must want you."

"What's the skit skit?"

Rob could barely speak, his mouth was gunked up with shock.

"The Grim Reaper. He takes different forms, like how you and I wear different clothes."

"He can't take you until you're truly, too far gone. You have to pr-"

The voice was cut off as the pterodactyl thing snapped him in its jaws, and flew off.

ITS TIME ROBERT LEE RUSHER!

YOUR TIME IS NIGH!

Sanatas tinev etadual

praise satan oh he comes now

Bells ring.

Rob isn't ready.

Hell, he isn't even considering.

"Oh, praise Jesus lord of Heaven God help me puh-leeze!"

Steps approaching.

Earthquake steps.

Scary wind voices running.

Invisibleroot sound rising,

like a tsunami gaining height

Rob saw thousands of little demons on the roof, all running at him.

One broke a window.

The skitter's claws smash through the wood door and wrap around Rob's belly, and yank him down the ladder.

He screams, praising God all the way down.

He paffs to the ground, unhurt.

The skitter rears back to rip him into confetti.
Kaji pounces him.
Rob breaks the mutt's jaw with the hammer.
"fuck ALL OF YOU!"
All the windows
doors
orifices
in the house break open,
every demon of Hell has come to eat him.
There are demon armies for miiles packing into the
house.
Satan is the big one, who maAAA!kes earthquakes
WitH his steps.
Rob says it.
and means it.
"I Love all of God's creatures, and beg forgiveness."
Everything pauses,
no movement.
A giant light flashes onto the house, picking him out.
The light sends him out the roof of the house,
flying into the paused world.
Where Satan is three thousand feet tall
(literally)
and has a human face.
(Rob sees that it's a mix, of the most despicable people
in history, every time he blinked a new face appeared.
Vlad the Impaler, Heinrich Himmler, Ted Bundy, a flash
of a horned goat every now and again with a couple of
snakes crawling through the head like sewing needles
in fabric.)))))))))))
Rob sees his house crumble.
He is shot up through the darkness at light speed.
He realizes he was falling the whole time.

And he was only feet from crashing into Hell.
And then a wild rush.
And he hits the top.
And smells soil.
He claws above him, not breathing, not seeing.
Hoping wildly.
Then his fingers grasp the top.
He stabs his hand through.
Then his forearm.
Then hands grab him up.
He wants to scream, but can't.
They pull his head out.
And he can see.
He is back home.
It's sunrise.
The pastor is pulling him out of the ground.
Shocked as hell.
Three police officers pitch in.
Soon his entire body is back up.
People snap pictures of him, reporters.
They murmur amongst themselves.
He looks at where his house was.
There is nothing, but a charred outline on the grass.
And a black hole.
"You okay Rob?"
"Who are you?"
Rob doesn't remember anything.
He remembers that he's now an avid Christian, he remembers that his bigoted past is now buried underneath him.
And that he lost his house and dog.
Kaji barks, in pain.

The old dog sprints out of the black hole and into Rob's arms.

Eyewitnesses would say the dog came out of nowhere. Whimpering with a broken jaw.

"You don't remember?"

"No."

"Well, let's get you back to the city. You've got quite a lot to do."

Reporters surround him, asking questions he ignores. He felt like a new man, changed, free, and a very open minded man.

He loved all people.

And don't you forget it.

Rob spun around, the sound coming from the black hole.

Laughter, and then a giant, skyscraper-tall forked tongue, slurp up into the sky, and nearly whip him as it receded into the hole, which filled with grass and dirt. And he heard laughing.

The Chased Immortal

The following is a series of personal accounts, reports, and claims made by men and women throughout history that have an odd correlation. If you happen to recognize or know of the whereabouts of the "Chased One" as one of his aliases is, please contact me at this number [cell number redacted]

2285 B.C.
<u>Excerpt from cuneiform tablet excavated in Iraq, 2012.</u>
On the sixth day of harvest, Anu had cast down one of his spirits, and had exiled him to live among us. In the morning, odd occurrences took place. The animals that bore loose, long hair had it rise, and stand up on end, and thunderclouds quickly came upon us. Lightning bolt and thunder crashed all through Mari, and the ziggurat temple was made to be a refuge from the wrath of the gods. Lightning got dangerously close, and threatened to kill us all. One tremendous final spark of light blinded all for a small moment, and the storm rolled away, as it came. When it has ceased, several homes were destroyed, and it was a time of great relief, but the fear had still gripped the children and babes, whose mothers clamored to calm them. Several warriors found the spirit hiding, away from the village, and brought him before the king. I, being the scribe, was also present before the gathering. The spirit wore garments of unknown origin, with cloth being stitched so intricately that it covered his arms, and that strange metal beads could pull close the front or open it. On his back, he wore a sack, not one of

bladder or hide, but one weaved perfectly and with strong material. His skin was an unnatural color, like the (moon) at night. He spoke in a complex tongue, with a syntax so abnormal it must've been the language uttered by the gods. All attempts by myself or the king to communicate and ask questions of his origin were not understood. He did laugh, and attempted to speak to us, only managing to say things such as "Nineveh" "Babylon", though he said these with an alien accent. The man painfully stressed one word, and tried to make it dreadfully clear, he kept uttering over and over "HAMMURABI" "HAMMURABI". Some soldiers laughed at him, for the way he spoke was amusing. After about an hour or longer, the man opened his sack, and revealed a small pot. He began to walk towards the stairs of the ziggurat, but the soldiers had their khopesh swords ready. The man tore a piece of the pot off and rolled it towards us. The soldiers, being awed by the pot itself, didn't prevent him from running down the steps of the temple. One soldier reached out and touched the pot, and it exploded with furious sound and a blinding flash of light. Everyone ran back and away from the now ashy, broken pot and hid in all corners of the temple. Only someone who lived amongst the gods could make the king and his veteran soldiers scream and bawl like children at the explosion. Like the thunder and flash of light before, the man had disappeared as quickly as he had appeared. Several slaves did see him running by their homes and out of Mari, in the direction of the (Tigris) river. A search party was sent out, but he was never found. The king has put it to record to say that the man was a trickster of the Annunaki, cast out of (Heaven) by Anu for thievery.

The king has also ordered that no further records be made and no more word of the happening be spread to other cities.

Excerpt from letter from Lucius Pullo, a Roman Centurion to his sister in Ravenna. This copy was found by a historical society in the 1800s and was carefully kept preserved in a library in Istanbul.

My dear Atia, the thousands of perils that surround me are too much to bear, I pray that this letter finds you by chariot or by whatever means I can muster. The godless barbarians who strike at the center of Rome know no mercy. I have seen gods run and fight in the streets alongside these (Visigoths). My legion had been routed, and we scattered to all corners of Rome. I was forced by several archers to seek refuge by Aventine Hill. There I found two men, demigods by the look. They wore clothing stitched with such intimate form, not robes as a Senator might wear, but clothes that attached to the body, with hoods, sandals reinforced with metal and other materials.

They looked to be soldiers, so I called out in the name of Mars, but got no reply. The men were clearly adversaries. One sported a black (hood-suit) and the other had odd (beige) clothes on, he looked like Mars. The man in black fought with fist and rocks, and "Mars" had deflected his attempts. They ran towards the city and I followed.

Barbarians ceased their pillaging for seconds to see the gods brawl. "Mars" was knocked off his feet and picked up a barbarian's blade, swiping it at the man in black.

They spoke in an alien tongue, but it was with great rage and fury that they spoke. The man in black was cut along his leg, but fought the same.

As more centurions arrived, the barbarians returned to their senseless murder. The two gods were unaffected by any other skirmish surrounding them, in fact, Romans and (Visigoths) alike ended up between the two and were killed in their battle.

But what truly made me fear, was the "god-weapon" "Mars" brandished. He removed it from its sheath on his hip and he squeezed his hand. This sent a volley of thunder and lightning through the air. Men once again retreated from the (block) at the sound. I took a safe distance and hid in a fountain. A projectile from Mars' weapon grazed my armor. At the end of their great battle, the Man in Black had beat Mars down into the pavement, and punched him until (he) shook no more. The man in black looked towards the sky, then spotted me. He smiled and said

"Veni, vidi, Vici. Et tu, brute? E Pluribus Unum!" He laughed as he said it, with his godly accent. The words still ring in my ears, sounding like random fragments of statements than the (laconic) speech of a (virtuous) demigod. The man in black ran past me and back to Aventine Hill.

As myself and the surviving Romans retreated to the Tiber, I remember a furious repetition of lightning strike and flash bathed the sky, all climaxing with one final blinding light. With it, justice had been served, and the gods were pleased with the victor. I miss you Atia, I shall hope to see you soon.

Virtus

I wake up screaming, knowing that Draconis is nearby. The headaches have arrived, the mild fever has set, the nightmares are posuit. I must continue on my path, or I'll join the Cavalry in the freezing depths of these mountains. I was always taught to remove armor when sleeping, but, in the hypothermic void, it keeps me warm. I sling the bow behind my back, along with the Claymore, slapped to my thigh on its bronze scabbard. The rest of my supplies I keep in my large, waterproof Nike bag, strapped to my shoulder.

I am delighted today, the blizzard has been sent south, perhaps my Draconis is as honored as my tutors assured me. The blizzard is not an issue from the temperature, but from the thin ice, from which I sleep, as I may fall to my death. But that is just fear incarnate speaking to me. Dragoons must learn when to trust the voice, and when to dismiss it. I take a quick look around, still seeing the mountains, still bland and white as an aristocrat, only shredded by the peak areas where the behemoths of ghost stories rest. The rocky path has been forded, by Draconis, and by previous Dragoons who have gone Virtus.

Father.

SHUT UP! Never remind me of it!

Had I moved another half-legion to his position, he would still be...

That's bullshit! You would've sent MORE men to be slaughtered with him.

I take a breath and forget it.

As I tread along the freezing path, every other step of my boot landing on cracked bones or rusted metal, I picture how the rest of my life will go downhill, as Virtus is the climax in the seamless continuum we call life. Unless I go Coetus Virtus, which none have returned from. Virtus, up until now, it just means traversing hundreds of miles through the Rockies. But soon, soon, I will be cooking Draconis back home, exchanging pleasantries with old friends and going to Officer Training. And maybe even marry Lenore, as many women prefer a man who has gone Virtus, then again, many women are disappointed, for such a man is seldom found fully unscathed.

Dad did it.
Will you shut-

He did it and his Draconis CAME BACK!

I bang my helmet to end the voice, it works.

They always told me that I would learn to adore boredom on the path of Virtus, but I rather disagree. Death by Draconis is preferable to ennui. I've read all the manuals they have given me, I've recited enough poetry to choke Lord Byron, I've fired arrows into the ice for target practice until the cows came home. I have nothing to do but carry my delirious body to Draconis for the last step of Virtus. My bloodlust is insane, I've questioned the possibility of pain, I contemplate suicide, just to pass the time! I would use my electric Equus, but the mountains are too thin, I would surely slip and fall to my death.

I watch the sun sail through the sky, and plunge into the West, as if the sun itself has escaped Virtus and hidden from his Draconis. At least slumber will bring excitement. I find a cave several miles away, and I trek over to it, just as the temperature drops 40 degrees. I lay my gear besides me, and exhaustion knocks me unconscious. Draconis sends posuit dreams into my head again.

America, the year 2134.

"No, do not show me again!" I moan.

The world is a buzzing telecommunication hotspot. Virtual Reality is reigning king of entertainment. The news plays a newnew psychological theory "Human beings are better off in the Middle Ages, where the mind is adaptable to survive, and bravery and honor are heavily accepted in society."
"They didn't... need to die!"

Then, Draconis came. They came from Bottomless Pits that originated from sinkholes deep in the Earth. Everyone, even atheists, believed it was Rapture. When

*hundreds of Draconis came out of the Denver Sinkhole,
Christians believed that they were going to heaven, that
Revelations had arrived, so they threw themselves at the
winged lizards, who in turn, breathed fire on them.*

The Denver Police were wiped out within an hour.

I scream. no sound, it echoes as if underwater.

*The Colorado National Guard was wiped out
within a day. Before the Military could react, there was a
sinkhole in New York City, when people looked down it,
they described it as a "black, empty void."
Draconis spewed from that sinkhole as well. New
York Resistance Forces were set up, even when they hid
in the sewers, they were demolished by Draconis within a
week. The Military struck with Special Forces,
recommissioned BLU-82s, and MOAB bombs and naval
bombardment. Casualties were Draconis: 5, Humanity:
498,073 by the end of the New York Skirmish.*

My training manual, oh how it saddened me
when I first read this.

*Then, the sinkholes started to open everywhere. The
Atlantic and Pacific Ocean was crisscrossed with
Leviathan Draconis, Europe and Asia were slammed hard
with green Godzilla like-Draconis, and the United States
were hit by winged Draconis (who were considered the
worst of all). After the smoke cleared, the year was
2140. Human survivors obeyed old legends, and homes
became castles, cities became kingdoms, and camo BDUs
were replaced with knight armor. And we called our new*

soldiers Dragoons, and they used a mixture of old and new weapons to defeat the beasts. After Draconis settled in the mountains, we realized that we should destroy their new breeding grounds. So we sent messages to oversea countries (by plane of course) to begin arming a Dragoon army. When the men were ready, we had a headcount of 2,000,000 Dragoons. We called this army the Cavalry, and sent them deep into the Rockies to exterminate all Draconis. But they were smarter than we expected. Their otherworldly abilities included altering Earth's atmosphere, the monsters created typhoons by thought.

In the aftermath of the weather and hypothermia, the new Cavalry headcount was now estimated around 1,750,000, but they marched on. When they finally reached Draconis in the Sierra Nevada, there were thousands. The Draconis were in mating season, so their species was more aggressive than usual. The bugle call was sent out, and 1,750,000 Dragoons fought to the death in the mountains. Back home, then people were beginning to think that the Cavalry were successful, a large Draconis plopped down a single man, with charred armor, bloodshot eyes and white hair, he babbled nonsense for ten years, and then he finally began to tell his story, the story of how the Cavalry was massacred until he was left. And he estimated that the number of Draconis killed were around 70. This babbling man offed himself shortly after telling his tale. His last words were begging no others to attack the Draconis.

I wake up screaming again, as the history of the fight is too much for the mind to bear. A blood-piercing growl enters the cavern. I look to my right and see a wild wolf, very large at that, and the worst part, he's hungry, as his thin stomach suggests. He pounces high, diving his teeth into my arm. I am unphased, as I have waited for an animal to kill for weeks. I grab its neck with my left hand, squeezing very hard. The beast is still at me. I am silent as it tears into the metal, causing only minor chinks to my armor. I overcome my bloodlust and throw the wolf to the other side of the cavern. I roar at it, my weary voice cracking between high and low pitches. As I gaze into the wolf's eyes, I bring my fists out, ready to pummel the mutt if it tries again. The wolf is weak, but submissive. It goes to the ground, begging for mercy. Amazing, the wolf has overcome the great Draconis mind powers. I'll bring the wolf down to the kingdom, then they can do research on it. For now, I'll bring the animal with me. So I grab a large piece of jerky and throw it to the creature. It gobbles it up fast. Then it joins my side, as if it was aware about my Virtus. The wolf trots along with me, and the blizzard hit us harder today, but the wolf still helped me, fueled only by the occasional salted meat strip. When night came again, I had the shelter the wolf in my arms for sleep.

I use a zoom feature on the fiber optics to notice an Inn, probably a 10 mile climb away. The icy rocks that surround the Inn are more like knives, preparing to slow me down at every step. I toss the wolf over first, then I get up myself.

I open the Inn door, noticing several barmen looking at me as if I am a ghost. "Coffee, 8 sugars, lots of cream." I say, exasperated. The barman doesn't say anything, he just complies. As he fetches the coffee, I take a seat on a fur sofa in the corner. The barman says "I thought you tough Dragoons took your coffee black, and with a side of hard bread."

I reply, pushing my anger into the response deeply. "I have been on the trail for three months. That's three months of climbing and sliding across the mountains. I haven't tasted "sweet" on my tongue since that time. So excuse me if my order sounds weak or emasculated, I just intended on returning actual calories to my deprived body!"

The barman says "I'm sorry, I, I haven't talked to a person for a long time. I just have a small chat with the occasional Dragoon that hikes up here, goin' Virtus."

I say nothing, as silence says a thousand words.

The man says "What is the name of your Draconis?"

"Dux Fortis."

"You know that means it's stro…"

"I know what it means. It is "strong leader"." I almost yelled. Silence again.

"How do you get your Draconis?" The barman asked, clearly attempting to break the silence.

"The Draconis chooses you. Every Dragoon receives an epiphany, and you see what your Draconis looks like. If you ignore the epiphany, you only get posuit nightmares until you fight back."

The barman hands me a light brown coffee, piping hot. He puts it on the table and I lift off my helmet, then drink.

"You're a brave man. I tell you, I wouldn't be caught dead trying to kill some big ass Draconis." I drop the mug onto a nearby table, and begin speaking.

"We all go Virtus. Whether we're just killing Draconis, or battling our own. There is no "chickening out" of destiny."

The barman smiles and looks up at me. "Boy, I was thinking of tying a rope 'round my neck and ending it all, but that really changes it."

"Why would you kill yourself?"

"Loneliness, I've been up in this mountain, serving Dragoons for fourteen years. And nothing to show for it but some white hairs and age lines. My Virtus is pretty damned sad."

"You haven't gone Virtus yet. I can tell."

"Aye? How so Caesar?"

I smile at the remark. He isn't the first one who's called me Caesar based on my looks.

"Because in the five minutes that we've been talking, you have shown your desperation to hide from Virtus. It still awaits you."

"Then what is it for me?"

"I cannot know. Only you can. Once it comes to you, you'll chase it until you're an old man, in Second Childishness. Then, your memories will be the true kings of the past."

The barman thinks about this, and then he smiles. "Thanks, Caesar. Not even me dear old Ma would get out of bed to stop her boy from killin' 'imself."

I finish the coffee and stand up to leave.

"Wait!" The barman yells. "Can't I get you something else? I've got hash, spam, what'dya need?"

"I couldn't dare offend you in that way."

"But, perhaps something to refill your food supply? You shouldn't go Virtus hungry."

I hesitate, then say "Alright, you've tempted me. I'll take all the jerky that you can supply me, and two waterskins."

The man dashed into his storeroom. He retrieved a giant burlap sack full of jerky. And two waterskins full of water.

"Take it all. I'll not need it for myself. Now I am proud to be lonesome."

"A quality of mercy is not strained." I say, smiling. Then, I bring the wolf over to the barman. The wolf sniffs him and accepts his company. "Keep the wolf. Now you have company."

The barman smiles and starts petting the wolf. "Buen fortuna Dragoon! Thank you so much!"

"Don't mention it. I've a Draconis to slay."

As I put my helmet on and carry my new supplies out the door, the barman asks "I don't think I caught your name."

"It's William. Named after the Conqueror."

I walk out the door, returning into the haze of the coldness around me. From there, I hear a tremendous reptilian screech off in the far distance, my Draconis is challenging me.

****

Days later, I have been caught in a second blizzard. I'll be damned if Draconis isn't annoying. Not even the mountain lions howl at night. Their weak, instinctive minds are under the control of Dux Fortis. As I continue on, I must expend a crossbow bolt or two in order to kill the lions in my path. The ground even grows warmer as I reach the Draconis nest. I am forced to sleep under snow and ice rocks, to avoid being hunted down.

The boy's training helmet gleamed in the morning sun. The horn call went, flashing the horse across the grass with precise fury. The boy's heart, the only part of him alive in the presence of danger, banged through his armored chest. As the opponent drew closer, the boy was numb, preparing for the inevitable strike, he closed one eye to center his lance's position. Then the collision hit, the boy felt the balsa wood lance of his opponent graze off the side of his chestplate. The boy's lance however, struck home near the opponent's collar bone. The opponent's feet rose from the stirrups for a brief moment, as if pulled into the sky by God, then the enemy flew backwards, into the hay bales beside him. The joust had ended, as abruptly as it began. There was a brief second of silence, and then, the small crowd cheered. The boy climbed off of his horse, ran to his dazed enemy, and removed his helmet.

"Are you okay Michael?" The boy asked, afraid. The opponent, shook his head, dazed, and then nodded.

"As good as can be William, but, please aim for the chest, next time, I don't wish to be choked by your lance's grip, only punched by it."

The boy William, smiled and lifted his concussed friend up, and they both did a salute to signify mutual

respect, settled their horses in the stable, and returned
to their homes for supper.

I wake up on my feet, my body ready to fling itself over into the chasm.

Dried blood and charred bones line the ground, as I trek through "Beowulf's Bay" the main nest for Draconis. My heart rate is very high, every single peek around my shoulder could be a speedy and painful death. The fiber-optic vision in my helmet glitches many times a day. I am nearing the end of my journey, which is both sad and comforting to me. I get an adrenaline high from this like no other event. As the battle screeches of the reptiles gets louder, I am forced to seek higher ground to survive. But as I dig my stabilizing pins into the ice to make my bunk to sleep in, I finally hear it. Dux Fortis's call. I heard it from my posuit nightmares. It is the sound of hundreds of people dying all at once. It is the soundtrack for descending into Hell, It is the devil's wild cackle, it is Draconis challenging me to a duel. On the 'morrow I shall end 'strong leader' and his sycophants. I laugh, broadly and with heavy glee, for I have found my poetic justice. My laughter synchronizes with the beast's, creating an odd unity that doesn't exist between foes. I even see, or hallucinate a forked tongue, hundreds of feet long, lashing into the sky on the horizon, and receding behind the mountains.

As the sun climbs over the eastern sky, the infant Draconis chirp, or rather snarl for their daily breakfast. I use thermal imaging to find Dux Fortis. He is easy to spot, for he is the leader, he is the largest, the one who is given the most food, the one who all the others back away from when he stares at them. Social hierarchy runs heavy here. There are leaders, they advise and lead their group to hunt. The females guard their young, along with the beta males, who are considered inferior. A Dragoon who has been selected by a beta Draconis is called 'weak' for he has a simple task. But a Dragoon selected by an Alpha, he walks with a tombstone over his head, for they are closer to Satan than to mercy.

I climb down the mountain, and prepare to get Dux Fortis. I wait for a half hour to find a small Draconis, he is the size of a fully grown lion. In order to not alert the mother, I use the crossbow. I shoot the animal in the throat, hopefully puncturing the vocal chords. The ploy is successful, but the victory is Pyrrhic. A brother to the small Draconis spots his friend in distress, and finds me. He does not scream to his mother, he charges me like a bull. His roar is lizardlike, he hisses loudly, and makes a guttural purr so deep, I can feel the vibrations under my skin. I drop the bow and pull out my Claymore. As the Draconis comes near, I aim for a bit of exposed flesh, then I jab hard, sinking the sword into the creature up to the hilt. It squeals, but only temporarily. The mother hears it and runs to her offspring. The mother arrives, her large head rears down to check on her babies. She screeches, it is so loud that the ground vibrates. The other mothers arrive. My diversion is complete. I drop down a metal ball, my Equus onto the ground. The ball splits open and becomes a horse, made of solid energy. I jump on it and the horse instantly moves forward. My mind guides the Equus. As long as Dux Fortis believes I am only thinking about moving, I will be safe. The Equus charges to speeds of 50 miles an hour. The beta males see me and growl, knowing full well what my intentions are, they dare not strike me, as their leader wishes to kill me himself. *Faster,* I think. The Equus speeds up incredibly fast, going around the bones and puddles of blood. I am past the beta males, luckily the Alphas have gone on a hunt. I see a series of creature-made caverns made to house the Alphas, and the leader has the largest cave. My hands shake at the thought of engaging Dux Fortis soon. I see the leader's mate, feeding her young from a large crevice in the cave, I zoom in to take a better look. I see that the mother feeds her young humans, whole. Some of them are people kidnapped from my kingdom. Draconis minds can brainwash humans, and send them anywhere they wish.

The Alphas are home, the sun is blotted out from their wings. I have snuck into the Draconis home and prepared to shoot with my crossbow. As Dux Fortis trudges into his cave, I gasp. Dux Fortis is red, not naturally, but red from bathing in human blood to intimidate the other Alphas. His eye is about the size of a shield. His grin reveals yellow, aging teeth, each the size of a pike. His face in general resembles that of the Gharial, a long snout and permanent grin. His mate gives him a welcoming coo, and Dux Fortis helps himself to the crevice of humans. He sticks his giant face in the crack and snaps up tens of men in a single bite. I can't help but think about the men. Dux Fortis hears my thoughts. He twists his head to my location and he roars. My position is already compromised, so I stand up to reveal myself. I light a flare, and drop it on the ground to illuminate the cave.

The shadows bounce off the walls as the red flare sparks shine off the monster's glorious fifty foot tall body.

"Soulless demon, I am here to end you through the ritual of Virtus!" I growl.

He laughs, like Satan might after cornering his next meal. Dux Fortis pushes his offspring and mate out of the cave with his tail. He grabs multiple humans from the crevice in his jaws, some of them impaled by his teeth. They scream and wriggle as he tosses them onto the ground, before they can scramble away, the creature launches a fireball from its mouth and ignites the men. Their screaming worsens as they struggle to remove their burning clothes from their rapidly heating bodies. It's a ploy to intimidate me, or to enrage me, unfortunately, it works.

I scream "You son of a bitch!" as I fire a bolt into the demon's face, the arrow breaks into a million splinters. I slide a second bolt into place from a drum on the weapon using my thumb. Then I fire again, the second shot diving home into the creature's chest. It stings the beast so hard that it drops to its stomach, where I charge it, luckily able to grapple on to one of his back plates. The Draconis shakes itself in order to get rid of me.

I remember my years of training, rodeos, we would do for weeks on end to strengthen our resolve.

"Easy knave! Hold back on him! Squeeze your legs into his sides!" It is the voice of my old master, as I struggled to ride the bull in the pit.

I awake from the flashback instantly.

I ram a short blade scathed with hemlock into his side. I am bucked off and I slam into the wall of the cave. The Draconis produces a fireball, again, and flings it at me. I jump to move, but the fireball is larger. It crashes into me. The fire washes over my body, along with panic. The fiber-optic lenses fail and fizzle out. So I lift my helmet off and throw it to the side. Steam rises from my near-corpse. The high- tech undergarment I wear beneath my armor cools me down. The beast shoots a thought into my mind. *I have chosen my Hominis well. You fight like your father once did. And you shall die just like him.*

Flashes of agonizing memory.

My father, leading the kingdoms of the West to a horrible stalemate against the Possessed Horde.

I was young then.
Barely 16.
Mounted on a fierce solid light Lupus instead of the Equus.
I remember the silent mutilation of my father against another Dux Fortis.
I remember the ear-splitting reception of his death in my screams.

Was, this the Dux Fortis? Who dared to kill my father? Who struck down Richard the Tiger-Hearted as he bled?
Yes. It is him.

Pure undying hatred bleeds through my wall of rational control. I pull out my diamond blade Claymore, dropping all other weapons, and strike him by slicing a spike off of his side, and stabbing the skin that lay beneath. The beast bellows in pain, crashing its claws into anything that looks like a human. I duck under and over his blows. The beast clutches me in his hand and strengthens his grip. I wheeze out all of my air and prepare to be killed.

An idea strikes my mind, *"The power of Christ compels you, demon!"* The Draconis hisses like a snake at my thought.

Dear Lord, bless this cave of sin, grace it and keep it and protect it from the swarms of Beelzebub!

A thunderclap sounded outside. The weather is being altered by the beast's agony.

The Draconis makes a gagging sound, as I think this. This would be Dante's favorite comedy. *Lord forgive my sins, I would be eternally grateful if Thou wouldst give me the strength to destroy this Satanic creature.* The Draconis drops me to the ground and whips me with his tail. I crash into a rock. I feel something hot at the back of my neck. I cup it with my left hand and use my right to swing a hook at the grounded Draconis' chest.

"GIVE ME THE STRENGTH OF SAMSON!"

God is on my side, as the punch makes a horrible cracking sound inside its body. Impossible, it's ribs are steel, indestructible, how-

The Draconis clutches its underbelly and whips me with its tail again. I fly backwards into the crevice. And I drop my Nike bag into it. The concussion makes me vomit. My mind makes me want to sleep, but I can't. It's definitely heavy brain trauma. Concussion, I won't survive the trip back. So I get up. The tail whips back again like a slave driver's. it slaps against my breastplate, leaving a permanent red scar emblazoned on the steel, and scours my cheeks. I nearly get whiplash from it, but I twist my body and roll with the whip, so my head doesn't snap back. Blood drips from my cheeks in two jagged lines. It whips its tail a third time, but I dive into the ground and the blow swings clear of me, and tangles around a stalactite. I bull rush the beast, bellowing not poetry, or rhetoric, but senile babblings, as I maneuver around the confused beast and jump, stabilizing myself on the nape of its crimson neck

I am David, and this is my Goliath, I think as I rip the plates off of the creature's neck. I use thoughts of weariness and concussion to stun the Draconis. When the soft skin of the creature is exposed, I punch it senselessly. Then I dig my hands into the skin, ripping it open. Dux Fortis flails its tail out, and bats me off again. As I hit the ground, I roll, absorbing shock and avoiding its claws. The sword, oh god, where is it?! My kingdom for a sword! Dux Fortis spots me, and emits a wail, of frustration, anger, perhaps even panic? I scream at it, focusing my thoughts to chip in on its psychological state.

It fails, as I can no longer hear his thoughts.
Never before in my life have I felt fear like this.
Dux Fortis' reptilian scowl changes. It bares its dark,
blood-stained teeth, and its eyes turn milky white.
I catch my breath, but I can barely sense it.
Dux Fortis leans back on its hind legs, resembling a
tiger ready to pounce.
The cave roof is more like a dome, akin to the
Pantheon, if he pounces, nothing would block his path
from crushing me under him.
I twist around, and sprint deeper into the cave.
I do not hear him jump, but I sense it.
The air pressure changes, I see a massive shadow fast
approaching.
Then he crashes.
The deep, echoing BOOM! reverberates throughout
the endless pitch black cave depths.
I jump with all my strength, just narrowly avoiding the
shock wave.
I roll and land on my back, no head injuries, thankfully.
If I can't eat you, then let the fear do it!
Dux Fortis' hollow rasp rattles in my brain.
The thunderstorm outside ceases.
I quietly get to my feet, attempting to feel for rocks,
walls, anything in the darkness.
The sky fades to black, now my only source of light is
the flare, seemingly miles away.
The Alphas outside the cave begin roaring. They can
sense that Virtus is almost over.
All I see is Dux Fortis clawing the flare out. I am blind,
weaponless.
But my opponent isn't.
I hear slight movements from where the flare was.

Shuffling, slowly exhaling.

Can you see in these depths, Draconis?

Aye, not perfectly, but enough to see you, bleeding from every pore, hands shaking like trees in the wind.

Our thoughts echo to one another.

We are both in pain, in fact, neither of us will survive, if I attempt to return home, I will bleed to death, and if you stumble out of this cave mortally wounded, your Alphas will spot your weakness and "overthrow" you.

I think to him, bargaining.

It's possible, but then again, death is the most crucial aspect of life, wouldn't you say?

He begins to monologue, the fool. I build a mental picture of the cave before the light went out.

My sword, must be, before the entrance to the cave, yes! I remember. I dropped it against a flowstone.

It follows and precedes life, and we mustn't let it catch up.

I had this conversation with your father, on the battlements, as he held his sword in both hands, terrified beyond belief. Just like you.

I feel the cave wall with my hand, and I slide across it, gently, telepathically holding palaver with the beast to distract him.

So YOU killed my father?

With pride. You know all hominis have different tastes? Has to do with the chemicals boiling in your heads that you call emotions.

Now a fool, tastes very zesty, tart.

For his head is seasoned with adrenaline, a chemical that springs from recklessness.

A lover-poet has a more sweet taste, for he is rushed with dopamine, a pleasure chemical.

The sword, must be near, I am approaching the cave entrance.

But your father, he tasted bitter, I took no pleasure, nor gained any satisfaction from eating him. I don't know what was in his head as he died.

My heart sinks, conflicting emotions bubble in my head.

Something draws air away from me just yards away.

I smell it on you too. Hopefully, taste is not hereditary.

I accidentally step on a pebble, and crush it under my weight.

I hear you too, O, poor hominis, your metal boots betray you worse than Judas.

I reach out, and feel tremendous ecstasy.

Its leather handle nests into my palm.

Draw closer, demon, let me have at you.

You've lost your mind.

Most likely.

I yank the submerged blade out of its stone prison. The ring it makes as I do this sounds like angels singing.

Please father, guide my hand, the beast draws near, and his voice is heavy with bloodlust, Guide my sword true, pierce this demon where he will be disarmed.

You will not slay me BOY! I am aeons older than you or your father! I am from an eternal realm, one you and your race will never understand! An ant there, but a GOD HERE!

I sniff out fear in his tone, or confidence, hard to tell sometimes.

I close my eyes, hold my sword before my with both hands.

I don't know if it was my father, or the savage shadow of instinct within all of us, but my body charged Dux

Fortis, and without the gift of vision, was able to bury my sword in its middle chest, up to the hilt.

Gurgles are all I hear.

Ah, yes, they taught us of your anatomy. I failed to pierce vital organs, but I did claim your ignition organ!

The ignition organ, lined with flammable gas, is what allows the Draconis to breathe fire.

Whether I killed him or not, he shall wander the earth forever, a forced pacifist.

He stumbles into the darkness, huffing and chuffing like a wounded dog.

I would never see him again. He could still be wandering in that golgotha, that endless black maze of cave tunnels, forever. 'Tis enough for Virtus.

The sky, bleeds blue again, and the night that was, disappeared.

The Alphas are shocked, they stop their howling.

The humans in the crevice come out and arm themselves. Most of their skin is gone, replaced by the pink, stringed muscle, and blackened bone. Their minds are still under control by the Alphas.

"Your father will still die with you!" The people say in unison, their voices inhumanly failing to echo in the cave. I wield my sword tight and point it at them.

"So be it. I have slain Dux Fortis, you are Philistines!" I stammer, my thoughts fragmenting as my mind begins to die. The men charge me, yelling. I hack into the first two without a second wasted. I suck in air to prepare for the next attack. I deflect one sword slash and more men stab me with short daggers. The blades penetrate the armor and I feel icy metal under my skin, a sharp, sliding pain.

"Bastard spawn!" I kick them off me and stab a sword wielder in the chest. I snap a man's neck and use his body to defend against the stabbers. I connect my right hand with a man's nose, breaking it off. I punch a man in the stomach and shove him into a stalagmite. As one man grabs my bow, I tackle him to the ground, disarming him. Never have I seen a point where a Dragoon's mind's requests exceed the abilities of the suit, and the red actions I order my hands to do are brought to full emphasis by the suit, and my fists move so fast as I punch the man, that blood rockets from his face and sprays all over the cave rocks. I grab the bow off the ground and quickly aim to one man, I pull the trigger and end his life. I snap to the next person and click the next bolt into the line, then I fire. All the men are dead. I stumble outside, fighting off exhaustion and nausea. I push Dux Fortis's head off of the cave cliffside. The Draconis' nest watches me with hatred. *Kill me then, you all hate me, then kill me!* I think. The Draconis horde all gallop at me. I don't care. In my condition, I won't survive the road home. I sprint forward and scream, swiping my sword at the Draconis all the way. *This place shall be my Alamo, and I shall be blessed of the opportunity.*

****

I use my Equus to reach Beowulf's Bay in no time. I don't see my Draconis, Fidelem Robustos, but rather several small Draconis, mourning the loss of their parents. I gasp, noticing all of the dead Draconis' bodies. Fire has scorched the ground, many of them starved to death and others ate one another. Some were stabbed to death, probably by another tough Dragoon like me who got a little too cocky. I reach the leader's cave and see William, his head ripped off of his body and his organs splayed over the rocks. The head doesn't drain blood, it has been cauterized at the throat with fire. His Claymore is plunged into a Draconis's eye, many others have been shot to death by bows. I estimate from a first glance, about ten males killed by human weapons, and female and small offspring killed by starvation. I kneel at William's head, he was my best friend, and now he's gone, just ripped apart on the Bay. Why would they leave his head? The horde spawned in Pandaemonium itself, had to leave its victim's head alive, to watch? To suck his soul out of his head? To preserve the brain and all of its weaponized knowledge?

"I'm sorry." I say. I ride back to the kingdom, with William's head, encased in a cloth bearing the kingdom's coat of arms. He has gone far beyond completing Virtus, and shall be legend soon.

Just like his father.

ABOUT THE AUTHOR

M. O. Beige is an aspiring everything,
lyricist/screenwriter/actor/director.   He is 18 and living
in Virginia.